MOKIE & BIK

Wendy Orr

illustrations by Jonathan Bean

Henry Holt and Company · New York

For Dad & Mokie-Anne, thanks for the stones —W. O.

For my sister, Emily —J. B.

Henry Holt and Company, LLC, *Publishers since 1866*
175 Fifth Avenue, New York, New York 10010
www.henryholtchildrensbooks.com

Henry Holt® is a registered trademark of Henry Holt and Company, LLC.
Text copyright © 2007 by Wendy Orr
Illustrations copyright © 2007 by Jonathan Bean
All rights reserved. Distributed in Canada by H. B. Fenn and Company Ltd.

Library of Congress Cataloging-in-Publication Data
Orr, Wendy.
Mokie and Bik / Wendy Orr; illustrations by Jonathan Bean.—1st ed.
p. cm.
Summary: For two rambunctious twins, living on a boat
means always being underfoot or overboard.
ISBN-13: 978-0-8050-7979-1 / ISBN-10: 0-8050-7979-3
[1. Twins—Fiction. 2. Brothers and sisters—Fiction. 3. Boats and boating—Fiction.
4. Humorous stories.] I. Bean, Jonathan, ill. II. Title.
PZ7.O746Mok 2007 [Fic]—dc22 2006011150

First Edition—2007 / Designed by Amelia May Anderson
Printed in the United States of America on acid-free paper. ∞
1 3 5 7 9 10 8 6 4 2

Contents

Overboard
or Underfoot

Mokie and Bik lived on a boat called *Bullfrog*. They lived in it, on it, all around it—monkeying up ladders
> and
>> down
>>> ropes,
over the wheelhouse and across the cabin floor.

"Twins!" their mother shouted, because the lines of her Art jiggled and jarred when Mokie and Bik played bumpboats—

bump thump rumpboats
up and down the wheelhouse,
bump thump rumping
from the steering drawers
to the bouncy bunk,
mump clump gumping
from sleepdog Laddie
to the potbelly hotter.

"Get out from underfoot!"

So Bik bumped Mokie out the door—*splat!*—into nanny Ruby's bucket as she was sploshing the deck.

"Twins!" shouted Ruby. "Get out from underfoot!"

Bik and Mokie monkeyed up the wheelhouse.

"Shh," said Mokie. "Mom's still Arting."

So they sunned like seals on the wheelhouse roof for about twenty hours till Ruby finished sploshing.

"Let's," said Mokie.

"Yes!" said Bik.

They monkeyed off the roof to the slippery wet deck, slip slide slippering in soggy socks, skate chase racing up to *Bullfrog*'s bow—Mokie was bigger but Bik was faster—and Bik balanced on his sliptoes at the very front point.

Mokie slip slid slippered back down the deck, skate chase racing past the wheelhouse, slip slide slippering down to *Bullfrog*'s stern, to balance on her sliptoes at the very back rail.

"Yo!" shouted Mokie.

Slow the tortle pulled his head in tight.

"Ho!" shouted Bik.

Ruby stuck her head out the galley hatch. "Be careful!" she shouted, because that's what nannies have to say.

"YO-HO!" shouted Mokie and Bik.

Slip slide slippering up and down the deck, crashing in the middle, thump bump crunch—Bik was faster but Mokie was bigger.

"Barnacle bells!" shouted Bik as he flipped over the rail—*splash!*—into the sea.

"Twin overboard!" shouted Ruby, jumping out the hatch, snatching her boathook, and fishing Bik out by his overalls strap.

Mokie and Bik were always overboard or underfoot.

Everyone Who Lived on *Bullfrog*

Mokie and Bik's father had a ship-at-sea with clouds of sails on five tall masts and a brrr-ooping broop for fog, and he salty sailed around the world.

He'd been on his ship-at-sea so long sometimes Mokie and Bik couldn't remember when he lived on *Bullfrog*.

"He's a parrot," said Bik. "He'll come home with a pirate on his shoulder."

"And treasure on his chest," said Mokie.

"He'll give me the pirate," said Bik. "I'll name it Jezebel."

"He'll give me the treasure," said Mokie. "I'll buy a botormike."

Mokie and Bik's mother had a botormike, with a little boat on the side. Sometimes, if Mokie and Bik were good as gold, she took them in the sideboat, roaring brrr-oaring down the road, wind knots in their hair, dust in their eyes, and spitting out flies.

But usually she just took her easel and her Art and sometimes Laddie. "Ask me no questions and I'll tell you no lies," she said when they asked where she was going.

Ruby looked after Mokie and Bik when their mother was botormiking or in the wheelhouse Arting. Rubies are like red diamonds. Mokie and Bik's Ruby had red hair and lots of songs but no diamonds.

"Hi, ho, the illy-ally-o!" Ruby sang when she put on the kettle for breakfast, and "I'se the bye that builds the boat, I'se the bye that sails her!" when she polished *Bullfrog*'s big brass bell and whatumacallits.

At bunktime when she hung her hammock in *Bullfrog*'s cabin, Ruby sang, "Now her ghost wheels her barrow."

The song ghosted through the galley, wheeled past the engine room, and barrowed into Mokie and Bik's cabin where their bunks pointed like an arrow at the very V of the bow.

Mokie and Bik's bunks had portholes over them to see the sea and drawers underneath to pull out like steps to monkey up at bunktime.

When the sea was calm, *Bullfrog* rocked them gently like a cradle. When the sea was wild, *Bullfrog* rollicked them—*thump clunk* overbunk—to the floor.

"Twins!" shouted Ruby. "What are you doing?"

"We overbunked!" shouted Mokie and Bik.

Ruby knew what Mokie and Bik were saying when nobody else did. She knew that cats were hissers because the cats on the wharf went *sss-sss-hiss* at Laddie. Fisk were fish, potatoes were tatties, and the illy-ally-o was a faraway sea.

"What *are* you yabbering about, Twins?" their mother would say, but most of the time Mokie and Bik were just with each other or Ruby or Laddie and Slow, and they could yabber jabber yackety gabber as much as they liked.

Laddie and Slow

Laddie was a sheepdog, a saggy shaggy, long licky-tongue dog with brown eyes hiding under his wool.

He licked Mokie's and Bik's fingers
clean when they didn't want to wash
and thumped his tail when they got up
in the morning—
    or jumped back onto *Bullfrog*,
    or when their mother's botormike
    rumbled down the wharf,
    or Ruby chopped meat.
Slow liked Ruby chopping meat too.
Slow was a tortle, and he was slow,
except for catching meat. Then he
was Fast.

When Mokie and Bik were buggy babies sunning on the wharf, Slow sunned too, but Laddie was a fierce "Who goes there?" dog and didn't let anyone near until their mother said so.

When they were crawling babies rollicking on the deck, he was a "No Twins overboard!" dog and grabbed their overalls in his teeth when they tried to crawl off the edge of the boat.

When they were learning-to-walk babies bump thump rumping all around the boat, he was a "Hang on to my tail!" dog, and they pulled themselves up and monkeyed over him and on him and all around him.

Now he was a sleepdog, still a saggy shaggy, long licky-tongue dog with brown eyes hiding under his wool, but he couldn't hear very well or move very fast.

"Laddie!" shouted Ruby when she was sploshing the deck and Laddie was snozzing in the sun. "Get out from underfoot!"

Mokie brushed Laddie's hair out of his eyes so he could see, and Bik shouted in his ear so he could hear, and they all skedaddled to the beach.

Laddie went to the beach every
morning and every evening to do what
a dog has to do, but skedaddling with
Twins in the daytime was sniff whiffing
treasure time.

Mokie found a green glass bubble
from a fisk ship on the illy-ally-o. Bik
found an oar with only half of it gone.

Laddie found a muck uck gucky,

sniff whiff stinky, long-dead fisk. So he rolled in it.

Ruby was still sploshing *Bullfrog*'s decks and singing "Hi, ho, back again!"

"What have you found, Twins?" she called.

"A fisk bubble," said Mokie.

"An almost oar," said Bik.

Ruby wrinkled her nose—"PEE-YOO!"—crinkled her nose—"YUCK!"—grabbed her boathook, and marched them back down the wharf.

"Laddie," said Mokie.

"Overboard!" said Bik.

Laddie jumped in and paddled up and down at the end of Ruby's boathook till he smelled like a saggy soggy dog instead of a dead fisk.

Slow was still sunning on the deck, and he still smelled just like a tortle.

21

Cowboys
and Captains

While Mokie and Bik's father was
illy-ally-o-ing, *Bullfrog* stayed tied up
to the wharf. Her wheel didn't spin to
push the rudder behind her stern and
steer her out to sea.

"Let's," said Bik.

"I'll be Captain!" said Mokie.

Mokie monkeyed up the drawers to spin the wheel, steering veering peering out the wheelhouse windows far across the sea.

"I'll be Cowboy!" said Bik. He monkeyed over *Bullfrog*'s stern onto the rudder to slip dippery ride a little bit on top of the water and a big bit underneath.

Mokie spun the wheel, steering veering peering toward the town where people lived in their houses-on-the-ground—like children in books, on streets with buses and trams and botormikes.

The rudder swung wide, swinging side to siding, with Bik clinging tight, slip dippery riding.

Mokie spun the wheel again,
steering veering peering out past the
harbor to where parrots and pirates
lived on their ships-at-sea, far far
away on the illy-ally-o.

She spun the wheel *fast*
  so the rudder swung *fast*
  swinging side to siding
  with Bik slip dippery riding
  splish swish sliding—
  splash!—overboard.
Bik grabbed the rudder and
monkeyed back up to be Cowboy
again, slip dippery riding, splish swish
sliding.

"My turn for Cowboy!" shouted
Mokie.

Mokie slid down to the rudder. Bik
monkeyed up to the wheel. He spun
the wheel fast, and *faster*, the rudder
swung wider, and Mokie was splish
swish sliding.

"Barnacle bells!" shouted Mokie.

"Twin overboard!" shouted Ruby,
and fished Mokie out.

Seagull Boats and Police Cream

Every morning, as the sun came up, when Mokie and Bik were still in their bunks in the bow, they heard Erik the Viking's seagull boat chug-chug-chugging out to sea while the seagulls squawk wawk rawked and Erik shouted "No fisk yet for pesky gulls!"

In the afternoon, when the sun flashed low on the harbor and Mokie and Bik were monkeying on the wheelhouse, they watched the boat chug-chug-chugging home with clouds of gulls behind her and silver fisk in nets on the deck.

When the nets were sad and empty, Erik was humph grumph mumphry thundercloud grumpy, and Mokie and Bik were good as gold and didn't run down the wharf to yabber.

But when the nets were shimmery
shivery fat and full, Erik rumbled,
"Plenty fisk, many fisk!" in a sunshine
song, and Mokie and Bik ran down
the wharf to see.

They stacked fisk into boxes to go
to market and sploshed the decks—
splosh swosh galoshing,
slimy blood and mucky guts
and icky sticky fisky bits.

The seagulls yabbered, "Mine,
mine, mine!" squawk wawk rawking.

"Plenty fisk for everyone!" Erik
sang, tossing slimy blood and mucky
guts and icky sticky fisky bits high in
the air for the seagulls to catch.

"Mine!" yabbered the seagulls.
"Mine, mine, mine!" and squabbled
back for more.

"When I'm big," said Bik, "I'm
going to have a seagull boat."

"When I'm bigger," said Mokie,
"I'm going to have a police boat."

Bik wished he'd said that first.
The police boat was the best of all.

The police boat was clean and white.
It didn't have clouds of seagulls or
decks covered with icky sticky fisky
bits, but its motor roared loud and it
was the fastest boat in the harbor.

When Mokie and Bik waved to the
police boat, the captain whistled his
whistle and waved back. Sometimes he
came alongside *Bullfrog* and gave them
police cream in a cone.

Mokie licked hers slowly, so it
melted on her tongue. Bik bit the end
off his cone. The police cream trickled,
licky trickly tickly, down his arm.

"I'll have police cream every day,"
said Mokie.

"I'll have a seagull boat for fisking
and a police boat for patrolling," said
Bik. "Then I can have police cream
for dinner and fisk for dessert."

When the decks were sploshed clean, Erik gave Mokie and Bik a fisk to take home—shimmery silvery fat fresh fisk.

"Yum!" said Ruby.

But when Mokie and Bik came closer Ruby wrinkled her nose —"PEE-YOO!"—crinkled her nose —"YUCK!"—because fisk is nice for dinner, but Mokie and Bik smelled like icky sticky fisky bits, and they stank.

So Ruby sang "I'se the bye that catches the fish" as she filled the big kettle on the stove, poured hot water into the bathtub, and rub-a-dub-dubbed them till she couldn't smell anything but soap.

Their mother got out the big black frying pan and fried the fisk for dinner.

Starfish and Sea Urchins

*S*ometimes Mokie and Bik didn't want to be together all the time every day. So one morning Bik untied *Tadpole* from *Bullfrog*'s stern and went rowboating.

Mokie drew a scotch-hop on the wharf. She scotch-hopped on her right foot, scotch-hopped on her left.

Now she had to scotch-hop two feet together to the squares at the edge of the wharf. It was the biggest scotch-hop she'd ever done. She wished she hadn't drawn it so far away.

Mokie breathed in deep, crouched down low, and scotch-hopped so hard... she flew straight off the wharf.

Mokie sank, sank, sank—

past the wharf's fat barnacled legs,
past the starfish and sea urchins,
past the surprised fisk,

till she could see the rocks on the bottom of the sea.

"Barnacle bells!" thought Mokie. She kicked hard until her head popped out—*splash smash thrash*—and gulped in air. "Huhh!"

But Mokie couldn't swim. She sank, sank, sank again—past the barnacles, past the starfish and sea urchins—and kicked and smashed and popped her head out again. "Whew!"

Bik was rowboating *Tadpole* on the other side of the wharf. He heard the splash and the *splash smash thrash*. He didn't know what it was, but he knew he had to find it.

He rowboated around the wharf as fast as he could and saw a tangle of yellow seaweed floating on the harbor.

Bik rowboated faster than he ever could. He'd never seen seaweed like that, and he knew he had to get it. He grabbed the yellow seaweed and pulled, and Mokie's head popped out of the water.

Mokie spluttered and spat out mouthfuls of harbor. "I saw starfish," she said. "And sea urchins."

She grabbed Bik's arm to pull closer to *Tadpole*.

"Twin overboard!" Bik shouted.
Bik's voice was loud, LOUD, LOUD—
that's what their father always said, and
their mother, and Ruby.

But their father was on his ship-at-sea.
Their mother was on her botormike.
Ruby was sploshing the floor in *Bullfrog*'s
cabin and singing "Hi, ho, the illy-ally-o!"
too loud to hear.

"Twin overboard!" Mokie tried to
shout, but her mouth was full of harbor
and she blew bubbles instead.

"Twin overboard!" Bik shouted
again, LOUD, LOUD, LOUDER,
but Laddie was too sound asleep to hear.

Slow didn't like Bik shouting, so he
pulled his head back under his shell and
didn't tell anyone.

Bik tried to pull Mokie in over
Tadpole's side, and *Tadpole* leaned over

too—tip-tip-tipping—and Bik was slip-slip-slipping.

The harbor started coming into *Tadpole*. *Tadpole* tip-tip-tipped more, and Bik slip-slip-slipped more, till he was nearly overboard with Mokie.

Bik held on to *Tadpole* with one hand and Mokie's hair with the other, and threw himself to the opposite side of *Tadpole*.

Tadpole sat back on the harbor the way a boat should sit, and Mokie slithered in like a slippery fisk.

"Huhh!" Mokie spluttered, spitting out mouthfuls of harbor over *Tadpole*'s side. Bik let go of her hair and rowboated back to *Bullfrog* because Mokie was wibble-wobbly, her teeth were chit-chattery, and she didn't want to go rowboating now.

"Ahoy, Bik!" shouted Erik the Viking, chugging to the wharf in his seagull boat. "What have you caught?"

"Mokie!" shouted Bik.

Ruby came out of the wheelhouse with a bucket of water to throw over the side.

"Twins!" she said. "Don't fall overboard while I'm sploshing!"

"I already did," said Mokie.

"I caught her," said Bik.

"I'll teach them to swim," said Erik.

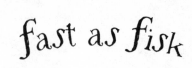

fast as fisk

On Sunday, when Erik the Viking's seagull boat stayed home at the wharf, Mokie and Bik put on their overboard suits.

"Mine's a too-cold-up-here!" said Bik, because Mokie's had a top and his didn't. They shivered down the wharf to Erik's boat.

"When I was a yunge," said Erik, "my far threw me in the fjord. 'Sink or swim!' That's what my far said."

"Did you sink?" asked Mokie.

"Or swim?" asked Bik.

"I sank," said Erik the Viking. "But then I swam, fast as a fisk."

"I sank too," said Mokie. "I didn't like it. But I liked the starfish and sea urchins."

Bik wished he'd seen the starfish and sea urchins. "I'm going to swim fast as a fisk too," he said.

Erik the Viking tied a rope around
Bik's middle and another around
Mokie's. He grabbed Bik and swung
him around, whirl whirr whizzing—
splash!—overboard.

Bik sank, sank, sank—
   past the wharf's fat barnacled legs,
   past the starfish and sea urchins,
   past the surprised fisk—
till he could see the rocks on the
bottom of the sea.
   Bik kicked hard until his head popped
out—*splash smash thrash*—and gulped in
air. "Huhh!"

"Paddle like Laddie!" shouted Erik the Viking and tugged on the rope before Bik sank again.

So Bik kicked his legs—flick kick swick—paddled his arms—splash pad muddle—and he didn't sink.

Erik swung Mokie around and around, whirl whirr whizzing—*splash!*—overboard.

Mokie sank, kicked, and popped up, and then flick kick swicked, splash pad muddled.

Mokie and Bik paddled out from the boat and back again, back to the boat and out again. Erik tugged on their ropes if they went too far.

Next Sunday, Erik tied the ropes around their middles again.

"I don't need a rope!" said Mokie.

"I don't need it more!" said Bik.

"Two Twins," said Erik the Viking, "and one Erik . . . and one angry Ruby if Mokie floats away while I'm catching Bik."

So Mokie and Bik filled their cheeks puff-full of air and scotch-hopped off the wharf.

Erik the Viking walked down the wharf with the ropes in his hand and a Twin at the end of each rope. They flick kick swicked, splash pad muddled, till their feet touched sand.

Mokie waded in to the beach.

Bik threw himself back into the water.

"I'm fast as a fisk!" shouted Bik.

Mokie ran back into the water and they both flick kick swicked, splash pad muddled, as fast as they could, with Erik the Viking running up the wharf behind them with their ropes in his hand.

Bik kicked so hard and paddled so fast, he went right past the end of the wharf and straight out to sea before Erik tugged him back.

Mokie stopped at the end of the wharf.

"I'm a faster fisk!" said Mokie.

"I'm a farther fisk!" said Bik.

"First fisk back to the beach is fastest," said Erik.

So Mokie and Bik pushed off from the wharf and flick kick swicked, splash pad muddled, fast as fisk, till their feet touched the sand and they splashed out of the water at the very same moment.

They turned around and saw their ropes trailing behind them. Erik was talking to Ruby at the end of the wharf.

"Fisk don't need ropes!" shouted
Erik the Viking.

"Who was faster?" shouted Mokie
and Bik.

"Fast as fisk, both of you," said
Erik.

But they both knew they were faster.

The Enormous fisk

Bik woke up so early one morning the world was still asleep and the sun was just climbing out of its bed in the sea.

Then he heard the seagulls yabber and Erik the Viking's seagull boat chug-chug-chugging, and Bik had a wonderful stupendously blunderful idea. He monkeyed down from his bunk and up the ladder to the deck.

The seagull boat was chug-chug-chugging away from the wharf and *Bullfrog* was rollicking in its waves.

Bik waved. "Wait for me!"

But Erik waved back—"Good-bye!"— and chug-chug-chugged out to sea.

So Bik got his own fisk line and
monkeyed down into *Tadpole*. Then
he tied the line to a ring on *Tadpole*'s
stern and rowboated away.

He rowboated for a long time
because the sun was coming up for
a wonderful stupendously blunderful
day. Suddenly, behind *Tadpole*, a
silver swish splash s-t-r-e-t-c-h-e-d the
fisk line straight and tight.

"Fisk!" shouted Bik. "I've hooked
a normous scormous eee-normous
fisk!" Bik tugged at the line, but the
enormous fisk tugged back harder.

Bik row-row-rowboated, and the
fisk tug tug tugged. Sometimes Bik
was winning and sometimes the fisk
was. *Tadpole* went backward and
forward in the middle of the harbor.

Then a ship brooop-brooo-oop-
broooped, "GET OUT OF MY
WAY NOW!"

The broop punched Bik's ears and nearly pushed him off his seat, but he held on to the oars and row-row-row-boated even harder.

The fisk tugged harder too. Then that normous scormous eee-normous fisk swish splashed out of the water in a slithery curve and tugged *Tadpole* straight toward the wharf.

"Thank you, fisk!" shouted Bik. Over his shoulder he could see the wharf getting closer and the *Bullfrog* with Mokie on the deck.

"Didn't you hear the broop?" Mokie called.

"A fisk hooked me!" shouted Bik.

Mokie saw the normous scormous eee-normous fisk swish splashing up to *Bullfrog*, with Bik and *Tadpole* a little way behind.

"Are you going to stop?" called Mokie.

"The fisk doesn't want to stop!" shouted Bik.

Mokie grabbed the boathook and ran to *Bullfrog*'s stern. She leaned out to hook Bik but the fisk tugged too fast, and all she hooked was the line.

Mokie tugged as hard as she could. So did the fisk. The line shivered and snapped.

Mokie fell over—*bump*—on her stern with the boathook in her hand. Bik tipped over—*thump*—on his stern in the bottom of *Tadpole*.

Then the normous scormous eee-normous fisk swam out to sea.

"I think it was a whale," said Bik.

"I think so too," said Mokie.

Sailors and Waggles

One fuzzy foggy morning a ship passed so close to the wharf that *Bullfrog* rollicked and rolled, and Mokie and Bik tumbled—*thump clunk overbunk*—to the floor.

The ship brooo-ooped. Laddie barked, Ruby grumbled, their mother muttered, and Slow pulled his head under his shell.

"I remember that broop," said Bik.

"No other ship comes that close," said Mokie.

Mokie and Bik monkeyed back onto
their bunks to stare out their portholes.
They could hear the ship's sails whooshing,
but all they could see was the fuzzy fog.

"Let's," said Mokie.

"Yes!" said Bik.

Mokie and Bik tiptoed out of their
cabin and monkeyed down into *Tadpole*.
They sat side by side, picked up the oars,
and followed the whooshing through the
fuzzy fog.

"Can you remember?" asked Mokie.

"Not really," said Bik.

"But it might be," said Mokie.

"I think it is," said Bik.

The whooshing stopped, and heavy ropes thumped.

"She's at the dock," said Bik.

They rowboated faster, and farther, until suddenly the sun chased away the fuzzy fog.

"Barnacle bells!" said Mokie and Bik, and they rowboated back a bit before they bumped.

The dock was so high and the ship so HUGE that *Tadpole* was like a flea beside Laddie. There were oil smells and tar smells, and parrots—

> whistling whistles and running fast,
> heaving ropes and groaning grunting,
> climbing masts and furling sails,
> yabbering and yammering.

Then the gangplank went *bang* and three parrots walked the plank to the dock.

"Is it?" asked Mokie.

"I think so," said Bik.

The first parrot didn't have a pirate on his shoulder, but he was carrying something that wiggled and wagged.

"A waggles!" said Bik.

The waggles wiggled out of the parrot's arms, overboard the gang-plank—*splash!*—into the harbor.

"BARNACLE BELLS!" shouted the parrot, and flung off his shoes.

Bik picked up the oars. The parrot threw off his hat. Mokie slid out of *Tadpole*. Bik row-row-rowboated and Mokie swam fast as a fisk.

Mokie pushed, Bik pulled, and a soggy waggly scrabbly shaggy licky round black waggles tumbled into *Tadpole*. Bik tucked it inside his pajama jacket.

"Twin overboard!" laughed the parrot, and even though he was taller than they remembered, and his laugh was louder, and his eyes were bluer, now they knew for sure who he was.

Bik rowboated to the ladder at the dock with the waggles in his jacket, and Mokie swam over and monkeyed into *Tadpole*.

The parrot monkeyed down the ladder into *Tadpole* too. He didn't have a treasure on his chest, but he hugged Mokie and Bik hard.

"I brought you a dog, a swimming rescuing Newfoundland dog," he said. "But you rescued him!"

Mokie and Bik rowboated home to *Bullfrog* side by side, with the waggles in Bik's jacket and the parrot in the stern.

Laddie barked, "You're home! You're home!"

Slow pulled his head under his shell. Their mother stopped pouring her cup of tea. Ruby stopped singing "Hi, ho, back again!"

"Twins!" they said. "What have you been doing?"

"We found a waggles," said Bik.

"And a Dad," said Mokie.

RUBY'S ROOM